The Sleeping Lady

The
Sleeping
Lady

JOE ROSENBLATT

EXILE EDITIONS

Copyright © Exile Editions Limited, 1979.

This edition is published by Exile Editions Limited, 20 Dale
Avenue, Toronto, Canada. Acknowledgement for financial
assistance towards publication is due both the Canada
Council and the Ontario Arts Council.

Exile Editions are distributed in Canada and the
United States by Firefly Books, 2 Essex Avenue, Unit 5,
Thornhill, Ontario.

Designed by Tim Inkster, typeset in Aldus by The Coach
House Press (Toronto), printed and bound by The
Porcupine's Quill, Inc. (Erin) in December of 1979. The stock
is Zephyr Antique Laid.

Second Printing. February, 1981.

Cover by Claire Wilks.

ISBN 0-920428-10-X

Nadine

Undulation from a sonnet — of spun milk —
lady eel moves on each slow rib:
iniquity vibrating low sound from a crib,
in gladness she flows — Uraeus in silk —
& coils contained as in a silent whelk,
tempt signateurs of fever within a dancing flame.
Her emerald eyes receive desert light
more settled than a lazy moonlit Phoenix
revived from rubescent embers, singing flight
where rills at evening flow in her brain.

More serpent than serpent in weaving motion
she absorbs waves under flowing skin,
tiny complexes trapped in circuitous sin:
— feline stirrings in transformation —
shimmering dance, O she's Mystification
thru our lookingglass — she raises her grin
above the Evening's sleeping mannequin
& dreams darkness in with its sick plutonium.

Lightly she glides into the soul's low bedroom,
voices bubbling: 'You've been here before
swimming in silence mooned in a white tomb
where teardrops vibrate on the warped floor,
Sweet Lady, you'd have made a lovely goldfish against the Gloom
dazzling a lunatic fumbling at the round door.'

Welcome to my parlour, diaphanous lady,
we've met before in another room
where silence nudged each corner cool & shady
& both our moons suffused as in a marbled tomb.

Juicier than eels, out of vapid air she eased
her feverish tongue ... turned its pointed love —
Like some pampered nymph, ripe & very pleased,
she lifted pure torso to her Maker Above

who dimmed her in a space between His eyes
where voices cried from deep inside: 'Paramour,
lie down in the parlour, bride supine, at moonrise —
we'll soon be stars ... part of the slime.'

Exposing himself in a warped mirror
limbless & vulnerable, a slinking traveller weeps
in a slow green melting hour ...
dreaming of pebbles, trees & intestines of the soil.

I think of serpents who've lost their skins
— a foil of morality out there on the snake farm —
the onanistic individual stained by Society,
matured, my fears are prominent in her nest.

Lost in a pestilential crowd of sobriety
segment by segment I fumble at a round door
only to find there's no keyhole there ...
& scaly despair slips into a deep waterhole.

v

Sailing into the sward's green suffusion
enamoured scribblers lose their virtuous skins
— tourniquets of love — unify in a slack season,
& trains swing, pierced thru by pins:
'Give us ligature enough,' pleads the interior,
'to secure the mind's trouser worm,
a segment honoured for its nature, superior,
yet longing respectability: — a tentacled form — '

On & on, rhythm in metallic ripples roved
until music cut a swath on hot dark waves;
into an easy weave our loquacious boa overflowed:
she followed a tongue of air — I crave
all her flesh suppressed into vermilion —
each ruby on her surface — an epithalamion —

As snakes matured their legs dropped off
& they slid away into that curious garden:
amphib Love, She pushed back the crowd,
limbs flashed mud from a previous fen,
those without scales fled rock & nook —
bubbled voice thru spawn & sediment
truth so potent that toads were cleansed:
'You who'd jump a spiral if she had hips,
glands are for thinking thru, not touching your disease —
follow a speedy sunspot to your lilypad
where flood-refreshed, emerge from bliss, be glad,
croak awhile at the sunset of your pre-existence
before His tears cooled down this pliable world.'

And what is flesh but a disguise
for women in narrow tapestries,
celestial gowns — beguiling skins?
Let us unzip this pure garment, unzipper,
allow the hipless flames to slip away...
again those legs they drop,
turn in a dry cistern
deeper than a hiss of Slumber's Serpent.
Touched by First Breath, the vibrating Lady
length by length, spills out a careful tongue
flickering thru leaves, easy spiral,
strips off her image. Her Majesty
pushed into a sinuous whisper — *yours in bondage*
an umbilical thought slinking among lost apples.

Lachrymal eel secretes passionate oil
to liquefy mirrors in that mesmerist
— soothes every pore of arboreal fetishist —
& urged into Spin by Love's shivering coil
those aroused ripples desire flesh to despoil,
as eyeball to eyeball in the cool Spiral
a low hedonist burns like furious coral
lost in the petals of glorious turmoil.

Paramour sheath scatters signals:
'lovers in the garden beware of My Spin
beguiled & beguiler live in a twisted thing —
stubborn as pythons summoned by Evangels
into undulant fire, ... they, the carbuncled, sing' —
burn! burn! scales! feathers! ... & unclean skin.

Moving its train past every dozing spectre
the spiral, an undertow oscillating
— tedious loop of piqued libido — tether
returning to an undisclosed centre.

A dangling convolvulus of silver
the land eel in sartorial moonglow
snares the mind's bruised apple,
towed back to Eden, & green hygiene.

X

Spasmodic eel sloughs off pure skin
— amorous sheath with legs trimmed off —
frost settles on limbs, pain, & kin.
He hears a lower voice in the water trough:
'Who lopped my branches on His Behalf?
May fiery opals ripen, prosper, & oppress —
Let venomous spittle corrupt sweet flesh,
O split tongue, darken my last seraph!'

Gown of scales, — wandering armour —
Sleep enclosed in her Serpentarium,
& opals dimmed on drowsy skin ...
slippery psyche, pet of my grim parlour
scatters glitter before a boa's Overseer
& silvered eyes of tortured Seraphim.

Spirals ache for hips, & limbs in delirium.
O Undulation, she devours our happy believer
who illumes crystal & mystical vapour,
for shimmer is gladder than goldfish in love:
— condensed essence, wafted above —
incorporeal splendor for Medusa's combers:
her tendrils writhe under pressure,
bubbles transfer Heaven thru verdure.

Step into the light, John, serpent light
motions your heavy sleep away for a broil
where tentacled selves about the self uncoil,
soul bird in an oven vibrating lignite
with a steady flame flicker out of sight
to settle in potent air, beer, & wormy soil ...
O bless our Chef in flambeaux of toil,
 — speed healthy light escaping in the night —
whose lovely arc purifies each kidney!
Out of the light, John, & avoid those tentacles,
your name's on every shot glass in a mirror:
'Hello, I'm Sidney,' the voice declares behind a glare —
& you reply: 'Make it a double, Sid, but easy on the ice'
& so that stranger drowns those minnows in your brain.

See you in the nitro-bottled future
— firebug in you vibrating luminosity —
& laughing deliciously in miniature
lost in slow smoke-rings of Infinity...

Sunnier than a mystic on his fertile bed,
spirit declares, 'No more lust but vapour
wandering over fiery icecaps, mist fed
to moonlight-eating connoisseurs of silver.'

Blindly we'll ascend thru a twinkling ceiling
feeding on dazzling uranium, — rising bread —
in sky where wiring's laid out for the dead
— all is cleansed, our Engineer is Sir Lucifer! —

The body you think you own is not your own,
is a rented tuxedo where you shine
like nuptial ants inside some pleasure dome
lifting molecules above their mind ...

Transporting glitter at your wedding
the self you think you own is your tuxedo
'til shadows lower it by parasol
to a beach polluted with tadpoles & panama hats.

XV

o ye that are born of lightning & methane
float on the surface
serpent in us plunge thru darkness
o ye that are born
again & yet once again
solar glow
hello
wild rose
labial fire
woe
let us drift

imploded sonnet fragment/undulation
o ye that are born of wild creation
let us glow again & again o hello
float on the surface ye that are born

In cesspools of love where trouble is deep
I got snakes in my head, got snakes in my skin,
woe so much pain from each spittin' flame,
into slimy waters these eels slip away

o ye that are born of lightning & methane
again & again your design blooms in my brain
attached to a navel, stuck deep in a drain
— hello Solar Glow, let's float on th' surface —

down in her Chamber I found myself drownin',
meandering shakers appeared with poison —
shimmying, they played out their misery
& they were familiar, & cruel, they were my own:

I had worn them to bed, weddings, & undulant memory
but they were faces lost at th' bottom.

Hello, you subtle substances
feeding hungry fissures at evening,
lend your glow to a sputtering lanternfly
dazzling in its terrible pool, staring at a Gape.

Hello, sunny substances, pulsing monitors
for others twinkling in their inkwells:
no footprints after night has
filtered thru the ceiling ... hello ... hello?

My salamander had no legs, no legs had she,
this busy eel climbed a ju-jube tree
after another limpid eel closeted in sin —
shining, she intoned: 'Life is such a whore
I'll go cool a different eel ...
but not *my* salamander, no legs for climbin'
tho she's a divil when her eyes flash to coal
& then little beauty swims thru every shadow.'

Air misty with snake musk,
brazen presence faintly undulating
reptiled back to hyperspace, — at dusk
released a voice into void, oscillating:

the man in a rubber suit waves goodbye
& salutes from a scintillated height
before creepin' into a cavity of his sky
turning out each & every pilot light.

— Hitman in a rubber suit out to terminate —
believes in rubber & power to erase ...
& finally when there's little shape, & no escape
his ozone bubbles on some dark surface.

'Friend, accept his nervous lady in your time
for she's a tassellated beauty, — yours & mine.'

Mystery, thank you for your necktie
I wear dangling to this country club
though it constricts at a supper show; sly
Nadine loops into my life for a slow rub

— Olivaceous lover leans against her oval door —
projecting sneers behind a smile: 'Sir —
use the tradesmen's entrance ...
you're too naked for my mystery tour.'

My visiting power lost, & she disdains a bribe:
I'd love to slither in — wrestlin' loveliness to the floor,
squeezing her narrow neck of pride, every bone,
since lovin''s a disease & she'd only plead for more!

Polyphony, o honey'd python, — yours is a lovely quagmire
where I've built a fire to dry out desire

Supple conduit surging thru musk
shivers as she U-turns in a pool
o lady with chartreuse eyes at dusk
in a season dry & cool ...

She's nude at noon
dreaming in an undertow of tongue
& her opals by their bloom
soufflé her, tumescent in her sarong.

Reposed in my consulting room
against this closet of private mind
she smooths out pythons of her swoon
tying easy rhythms with each line.

Chartreuse tongue on prowl
minnows under skin — advances, & retreats.

In darkness she grew a narrow flame
cool at evening, fired up at dawn,
lost eyes slept on her lawn.

At noon she played twisted games,
eel upon eel sailed in her schools
'til heat spiralled from the sun.

'Who will ye pass time with in th'sky?'
— an inflow whispered in His shade —
'with you,'said I, 'o lady of lupine pools,

o I found thy shy body hidden in its sari
hssssssssss ssssssssssss ssssssssss
under th' belly of subtle letter: - 'S'
asleep, my skin is greensward hsssssss'

Further out than prayer
meandering, she bequeathed a rib
while rippling billows clung above
drowning in th' air... o twisted love
she moaned, & moaned in bed
her see-thru nightgown shook th'stars
— torso quivered like a flame —
about to touch a moth
& all the shingles
shivered on her skin.

There was a turn by name of easy virtue
doin' tricks in zoos of incongruity: it was cruel,
she was cool sliding off her gown, ice —
stretching like one who'd meant to stretch ...

'Lotus material,' mouthed her agent, 'fluid on camera ...'
An honest printout diminishing lesser auras
beads glistening on his domed forehead
beads of gold ... he was a movie mongoose —

There was a turn by name of easy... & she did tricks
for sightless psyches: braille striptease
in a blind pig where sewer gas burns away
& all illusions flow into one Nile.

Let's buy you a drink, sweet woman
you're smooth but you got no apples
just tongue & tapestry
meat packed to boogie your night away.

'You there, ever pump snake?
they're so clean, re-shingles, every time.'

XXV

Transplants of thought
swallowed whole,
munch your leaves
leaving prefungi residue
for mushroom miners,
— love's honest —
under this earth
we'll meet glow worms
of our future.

XXVI

Absorbed, tubular, & alone
I slither along the beach after a room
'til neon flickers in my brain — vacancy —
& fireflies assemble in another tomb.

My spirit returns each angry bloom
feeding on moons, letting my body grow
where eels dig in after dark
I push away the glow.

XXVII

Some snakes are plated
others sway in tweed
molested
on love's table
where digestive
juices dry.

Praise Him to dim
wraiths shining in our bed
if there are snakes
then toads are quaking
in that bedroom
with faces warm as milk

Snake eyes thru th' night
a staple diet of stars
— our phosphored maitre d' —
sends regrets
for those who failed
to phone for a table.

Fingers flambeaux
to our pond:
into th' darkest well let's pour
those worlds & start again,
some snakes have plates
others sway.

There was a young woman called rose
who lived in a garden of repose,
when the moon was full bloom she floundered unglued
& grew on the outside into pulchritude.

From tip to tip she reeled on prowl: — required
mottled desire fused with luteous fire.

There was a flaming nymphet called rose
fluent with mildew, toadstool, & woe,
her mouth lipped tones of noxious psyche
while soul whistled an eel's miserere.

That tune was dry ice — o when moon was in bloom — within
plausible tapestry, a lover she enclosed —
& luxurious rose lapsed into sin,
fresh femme from a bog of enchantment,
all lips & laughter ... succumbed, to His Lament.

A hot humid day, my soul on the lawn
 — nubbly mouth cruising, any small animal —
'Try filet,' whispered the greensward,
'even a garter snake goes for mice in his sleep.'

I'd been a cool comber blinking at the sun
when my coat peeled from its delicate frame —
exposed, those small bones darkened — I was done —
meat meat ... soul shrieked: *meat meat*

& how could I resist a cry from soil?
I was the game ... my dust ... my powder ...
'Meatless day,' it sang, 'nothing to eat ... eat ...
I shall suffer no other Transmutation before me, — but meat ...'

Friends, no glow in my poem, or above it
but on mildew'd day He'll write your bloomin' sonnet.

XXX

Break the chrysalis, babe, don't be shy
break through the gauze & viscous webs,
I'm shining in on the outside ...
illumed, your skin's asleep, flows, ebbs ...

Princess, you've matured too long in your bulb,
be my busy moth, & I'll be combustible,
break out, flutter awhile, probe each lightbeam —
I'd say that chrysalis is beautiful, & clean.

Fantom, I'm food for luminiferous machines,
at midnight I'm roasted, inflammable,
tentacled by intelligence, hauled below, reamed,
where failed sunsets & sonnets bubble:

'Why be afraid? break out! break out!
o see those leaves fade before greater incandescence.'

o for bog terrarium with spring peepers
singing to a body retiring in peat moss,
there to wander after palpitating leapers
devouring minnows of thought in process.

Some snakes climb trees, I climb within
crevices spilling fermentation's fume —
spiralling out & in, never tiring of spin
I beg my Keeper to play the same rising tune.

Before releasing Lady Nature's Signateur
they renounce their final skin as invalid;
sibilating into green investiture:
coupling snakes, embarrassing in salad.

Mistress, forger, she's all wreathen pestilence,
blots us groundward for symmetry, & consciousness.

XXXII

Small green boa swam the high branch
for he'd heard there was pig on a limb —
tubed out in transit, — hot for fast romance —
motioning sylph, birds, & neighbouring kin.

Pushed against moons: sweet meats, diseased —
blooming more shine than Devil's own Compost,
'Only the Beginning,' he wheezed thru ju-jube leaves;
submerged in deep felicity, youth raged at meadows

where cool tubes sang to spreading sparrows
who fell into pools: — slumber their song, & food,
while under soil Desire snouted truffles; sorrows
inched, grew into stone, — fate of its brood —

leaving a memo for svelte reader, but no moral — anywhere:
'... dry here in the well, little boa, could you spill a tear?'

XXXIII

I shall importune the blind white ghost ...
fill her bowl with milk dreamier than snow.
— snakes love milk in lieu of lachrymose —
& I am cleansed by her alabescent glow.

Recumbent on a limb in my terrarium
Nadine lunched on a golden toad leaping air
excepting One who unzippered a gyrating rhythm:
— whose webbed fingers dimmed his own flame in despair —

Dressed in scintillating moonlight
she shimmered after straddlers out of lust
& flowing in a stream her eyes bloomed night
closing their silver on an eel in dust.

Temptress Nadine, some ice-worm'll visit you this Winter —
our reflection's shattered in every shard, & splinter.

XXXIV

There was an awkward creeping of flesh
with every contraction of her frozen hood;
tossed into circles, creature in distress —
she whistled for melody's low mood food

lurking, half floating, by circumnavigation
her flow enticed straddlers from a local well
to Imperialism's Tube, — bulbous hibernation —
& designed by petite Nadine: — a slender Jezebel —

bulged plump aqua-dweller, cool as obsidian:
'Length of passion, gaze upon this prize
for it complements th' fire in your eyes,
kiss away hallucination, free our amphibian!'

Sonneteer, stare at that webbed stranger on my lawn,
study this messenger: are we not issued spawn?

My blood becomes coal,
darkens my body inside a shiny tomb:
'Hello, hello, my sonneteer,' Snail cries:
'Time for vibratin' in th'shade
feedin' escargot in clay
as though It intended to stay:
don't throw away a bubbling snail —
that house she carries is your own.'

Lifted jaws emit sounds of protracted glory:
Nadine's having clever dreams tho nobody's home
when thermal tubes lure thee thru the open door: — *memento mori* —
& that rustlin' gown's th' final sound before a moan.

Lover, I had dreamt of dewdrops on my lonely bed —
a prisoner convulsing in his cyanide chamber
& I thought of you, Nadine, — inhaled your musk, instead
memento meri — Life's furnished in plates of heavy armour —

A dream's outside my stony door lookin' in
at tubes retreating into commodious domicile:
& those faces you adore release their grin,
lie in state, reposed with Love's diseased bile.

Dartin' right & left, she's prone to worship Sinuosity,
vibrating tongues at her Graven Image, out of curiosity.

XXXVII

Of strenuous folds disengaged below, – & sibulation above,
matured, disease-free: 'memento mori' or 'memento meri'
ah ... Nadine unwinds where serpents love to bathe,
monstrous to behold, encoupled by the heat they carry.

... My rat-self bewildered in lovin' cage, engaged
vipers in their rolling dance 'til I fell in a tapered trance:
this long lean breathing tube of shingled rage & shame ...
& o, that Undulation was too hot for perforation – so it seemed.

Madame inclined her neck of pride in vitriolic air
& reviled her public by the progressive movement of her hips
(– those ribs, of course, pursed in pairs –),
while she listened thru skin for the concord of sweet sound!

'You,' she spewed, 'destitute of limb, take heed –
don't emerge too soon, take all th'sweet time you need.'

XXXVIII

Go renovate thyself, Nadine, rid yourself of pleasure skin
you're more voluptulip in nakedness than Love
whose sleeping rose lies hushed below, — or above —
tongue to tongue, — Nadine moons up a fly of thought —

despair in veiled bedrooms of her flesh,
pleasures for my addiction, bless —
bless every bite: punctures deep & bright,
& fevers at the root raise up my flame again, Nadine.
Thy redolence purloined is wafted to my brain
wherein humbled spirits bequeath a benediction:
'Go renovate thyself, & Death ... o strip away...'

Rattling at night they invite Nadine into my dark
whilst unclean reptiles climb lichen-covered bark.

XXXIX

Touched this emerald, beam of wild serpent —
passing shimmer on th' lawn before time's spent
this sullen creature all alone; I know
she wears anger as one living an Afterglow:
'If only I could loosen the cartilage in my jaw...'

Weeping softly, more treasured than ravished,
Nadine tubed out on the prowl — erupted on route,
leered into verdure, & then, disappeared —
for what she offered was too warm to keep.

Lost on a slope, — greensward of my sleep
sensual, yet frozen beneath ... delirium —
Nadine iridescent beamed her way,
luring me home on a silverous day.

I'd a night dream, my wet lovely,
so unctuous, I slipped my skin in awe —
a smooth eel sidled along your body —
teased that stranger in th' raw

I'd a dream before I dreamt Nadine —
that eel extended himself between her thighs,
moistened little-rowboat-man in-harbour
she chilled him with her lips ...

I had Nadine in my serpentarium:
in another world, in First Menses, o Spirit Child,
Omen swimming in some mottled Nile
at th' bottom, driving water serpents wild

— smaller than a tear — & spilled by a careful hand,
Nadine, I drink liquid sleep black as your basalt heart.

XLI

On elongated rib Nadine slid, mouth agape: —
'My coils are tightened to stop life, not crush —
darling we live in perfumes we've made
wherein we vaporize in a terrible rush ...'

o when Nadine smiles she'd stop a water-clock
instead her Freeze is on the blood pumping in my heart
for Love has left her tender clutch: — fertile stock —
on moss, or any mound, where souls disembark.

Whistling my name she looms above th' Gloom
against St. Elmo's light, dancing in that fog
& U-turns in the evening tossing up spume;
deeper & deeper I'm into her slimy bog.

Down to th' spot where snakes climb out to please —
they move on elongated ribs, Lovin''s their disease.

XLII

Toads at sunset blink into Mephisto's fireplace
'til they feel round as apples in the heat,
 — o clowns souffléd with elevated eyes — embrace
as they tumesce inside their tubercules of meat

absorbing ozone as tho the 'intire' skin was flame
or some flag, inflated, for the batrachian
sweet travellin' bag of webbed desire, & shame,
spawn & I submerge for thee to where it all began ...

Rejoicing in a tadpole's iridescent flight
& coalesced into that tribe of vibrating essence
we sing to breathing mud lumps in their twilight
where every straddler has his lurid incandescence —

'Push off,' intones Nadine gliding thru the flue,
'I've tanned my dark side by th' fire, so must you.'

XLIII

'I want to be Seas of Hydrogen whistling to th' Element:
Light me up, honey, I'm here for explodin'
Listen, Intercessor for Combustible Gas & Arboreal Hygiene,
sure, your fire snakes mingle in coral, infusin',
they sing, coupling aisle to aisle
releasing umbilical signals from their furnace — '
Nadine, petite in th' bush, freezes a smile
& puts on the squeeze to warm a crevice
whilst all her apertures liquefy —
Snakes pretend to listen to birds & their urge
& so that sinuous force lurks high in the bush
devouring a melody & feathers, heavier than dirge —
Snakes love birds — both lay eggs — but one's ligateur:
she ties both ends about th' middle — our signateur — ?

XLIV

Looks like snakes in th' rain & fish in th' sea
Yeah, there's a snake every day new as prayer,
there's snakes in water without my good shape.
Pull me forward o shimmying whore in the air,
looks like there's serpent everywhere o & you gape
eatin' life forms most small, humble, sensuous —
How you doing out there, boa constrictor — lust?

Subsuming to an earthworm in a greenhouse,
dreaming I'm muscular & it isn't wet, but dust —
All men must face that Maker of our Inanity:
Snakes in water imagine it's wet & mellifluous
is only a word an eel could whisper —
Now a stick lyin' on a river bank could be a shaker
but then we could be dead, or on th' make for our Maker.

XLV

Toads are valuable in greenhouses, — I'm not —
on rainy days they'll eat a slow dew worm
slipping out to avoid drowning, or they'll rot —

Toads lie low for a turn, to touch th' squirm ...
dull grey sentinels with warts of wisdom — age
spews on worms' vibratory music, & sweetly fades.

Toad wears a jewel on his head to hide his rage
& he'll gaze thru that stone for th' hate he's made; —
it seems I'm pushed thru air by a lightbeam:
today there's lots of snakes in th' rain lacking my shape,
tho they look like fish meandering through a clear stream
where old Stretch sleeps over his Gape.

Sometimes a shadow looks like a water snake, or undine —
O when it rains, do your worms come out to sing, Nadine?

Date Due
